FRANKENSTEIN

Published by
RABBIT ROOM PRESS
3321 Stephens Hill Lane
Nashville, Tennessee 37013
info@rabbitroom.com

Performance rights are neither granted nor implied.
Contact info@rabbitroom.com for information on performance rights.

Cover design by MA2LA

ISBN: 9781732691018

Printed in the United States of America

FRANKENSTEIN

STAGEPLAY ADAPTED BY A. S. PETERSON

Also by A. S. Peterson

Fin's Revolution

Book 1: The Fiddler's Gun
"A soulful, instant classic."
—Allan Heinberg, Screenwriter of Wonder Woman

Book 2: Fiddler's Green
"Inventive, engaging, unpredictable. Peterson's prose sparkles with life."
—Douglas McKelvey, author of Every Moment Holy

The Battle of Franklin
Original Stageplay
"A true poet, Peterson's language is rich with imagery."
—Amy Stumpfl, The Tennessean

Tales of an Unremembered Country

The Timely Arrival of Barnabas Bead

The Oracle of Philadelphia

Cast

OLD SAILOR – a grizzled old sea hand (40s–50s)

YOUNG SAILOR – an inexperienced young man (20s)

SAILOR 1–3 – the company

CAPTAIN WINTHROP – an experienced captain & explorer (40s)

VICTOR FRANKENSTEIN – a young nobleman (30s)

ELIZABETH LAVENZA – "cousin" to Victor (20s-30s)

ALPHONSE FRANKENSTEIN – elderly father of Victor (60s)

WILLIAM FRANKENSTEIN – a young boy, brother to Victor (8-10)

JUSTINE MORITZ – governess to William (30-40s)

THE MONSTER – Victor's creation: imposing, scarred, hideous

AGATHA – a young woman, wife to Felix (20s)

DE LACEY – blind and old, father to Agatha (60s)

FELIX – a young man, husband to Agatha (20s)

JUDGE – an old man in magistrate's robes

VILLAGE WOMAN – a shopper in the market

BAKER – a middle-aged man or woman

PASTOR – a middle-aged man in 18th-century Calvinist dress

DRESSMAKER – a middle-aged man or woman

CAROLINE FRANKENSTEIN – mother of Victor (40s)

INSPECTOR – a middle-aged man

ACT I

SCENE 1

PROJECTION: The High Arctic – 1799

The stage is set with the railing of a ship and a mast. The cast enter as sailors. Each member carries a log of wood and piles it by the rail.

OLD SAILOR: Wrap that coat up, sailor.

SAILOR 1:   Aye, it's another cold one.

YOUNG SAILOR: It's always another cold one, innit?

OLD SAILOR: Pile that wood on deck. May be the captain will allow us a fire in the stove today.

SAILOR 1:   Hear that? We'll have a fire if we're lucky.

SAILOR 2:   We'll be froze solid if we aren't.

OLD SAILOR: Get up now. Move. It's our watch.

YOUNG SAILOR: You heard him. Get up!

SAILOR 3:   *(sarcastic)* Aye, we might miss something.

SAILOR 2: Miss what? Another day of exploration and adventure?

YOUNG SAILOR: We ain't explored nothing but ice and wind that I ever seen.

SAILOR 1: I seen plenty of that back in Halifax.

OLD SAILOR: We do as the captain says, and we do it pleasurable, see? That goes for all of you. You too, Obadiah! We'll find warmer wind soon enough. Set the watch!

YOUNG SAILOR: Set the watch, aye.

The Young Sailor hangs a lantern on the mast and rings the deck bell.

OLD SAILOR: Well? How does she lie?

YOUNG SAILOR: Like she's dead under my feet.

SAILOR 2: Held fast.

The sailors peer over the rail.

OLD SAILOR: Aye, she's ice-locked still. But no matter. She'll come alive soon enough. Just you keep your watch and keep quiet.

A sound like a man driving dogs.

OLD SAILOR: What's that?

YOUNG SAILOR: Something's out there!

OLD SAILOR: Look! Below that ridge of ice.

SAILOR 3: Is that a dog sledge?

OLD SAILOR: Something odd about it.

YOUNG SAILOR: Something damned eerie, if you ask me.

SAILOR 1:   Nothing can live out there.

OLD SAILOR: Aye. You go on now. Rouse the captain. He'll not
                want to wait till morning to hear of it. Go.

YOUNG SAILOR: Aye.

The Young Sailor exits, shouting.

YOUNG SAILOR: Captain Winthrop! We've seen something out
                on the ice!

The Old Sailor runs to the edge of the stage.

OLD SAILOR: What's that?

He stares out into the audience, looking and listening.

OLD SAILOR: Father in heaven!

*Victor enters, stumbling toward the stage from the back of the the-
ater. He's clad in an enormous fur coat and is pulled aboard by the
Old Sailor. He collapses in exhaustion.*

OLD SAILOR: Sir, are you well?

VICTOR: Have you seen a sledge pass near?

OLD SAILOR: Aye. A moment ago. Or else it was a phantom of
                the ice, a trick of light and shadow.

VICTOR: He was no trick of light. And no phantom either.

OLD SAILOR: Come below, sir. Let's get you warmed and fed.

VICTOR: Unhand me. My quarry does not relent, and
                neither shall I.

OLD SAILOR: My captain will not allow you to perish. Come
                 below, sir.

                 Fetch him something to eat!

*One of the sailors exits. The Young Sailor and Captain Winthrop
enter.*

YOUNG SAILOR: Thurston seen it first, sir.
                 (shouting to the crew)
                 Captain on deck!

CAPTAIN WINTHROP: I am Captain Nathan Winthrop, and this
                 is my ship. Come below, sir, and let us tend you
                 in warmer quarters.

VICTOR: Before I consent to remain aboard, tell me where
                 you are bound.

OLD SAILOR: He aims us north, and for near on three months
                 now.

VICTOR: North? What errand drives you to this desolate
                 place.

A sailor brings Victor a bowl to eat from.

CAPTAIN WINTHROP: The Pole, sir. We seek the North Pole and
                 whatever passages lie beyond.

YOUNG SAILOR: And "all the fortune and glory a discovery of
                 science affords."

VICTOR: Then we are the same, you and I. We share a taste
                 for the fruit of hidden knowledge.

CAPTAIN WINTHROP: My taste is for the betterment of mankind,
                 and for the advancement of science.

VICTOR: As was mine. A golden vision I once had, though it is long-since dimmed.

A shadow passes across the ship and dark laughter fills the air. The sailors shout and look out over the ice.

THE MONSTER: *(offstage)* While you live, my power is complete!

Victor thrusts the bowl of food back into the YOUNG Sailor's hand.

VICTOR: Listen to me! I had hoped the memory of my sins would die with me, but for your sake I shall reveal my misfortune.

Victor climbs to his feet, as if the thought of passing on his secrets has invigorated him.

CAPTAIN WINTHROP: Be at ease. A good tale will serve us all well, but let us speak of it in my quarters.

VICTOR: Were we among tamer scenes of nature I might fear to encounter your unbelief, perhaps even your ridicule, but many things will appear possible in this wild space which otherwise would provoke doubt.

The shadow passes again beyond the ship and the sailors shout in alarm.

THE MONSTER: *(offstage)* Come, my enemy! We have yet to wrestle for our lives!

VICTOR: We have little time. Come. Come closer, and hearken now. The fate of Frankenstein unfolds.

SCENE 2

As Victor speaks, the ship transitions to Victor's lab. Victor removes his coat. He is no longer disheveled, but a well-dressed young man. He points into the distance (offstage).

VICTOR: A creature approaches. A being of intelligence and vigor and strength. A figure in whom all my dreams ought to have been realized, and yet in whom all my hopes have perished.

Elizabeth enters. The scene change is complete and Victor has a cat dissected on the table.

ELIZABETH: Victor, there you are!

VICTOR: Elizabeth, you must save me from the stupidities of the academic mind.

ELIZABETH: I thought you were enjoying your studies.

VICTOR: *(holding up a book)* This imbecile could not uncover a revelation of science if it lurked in his own bed sheets.

ELIZABETH: Surely it's not as bad as all that.

Victor continues alternately searching through books and studying his dissected cat.

ELIZABETH: What is this?

VICTOR: It was only a stray. Justine has been after me to
                get rid of it for a week.

ELIZABETH: Somehow I doubt this is what she had in mind.

VICTOR: But look here. Do you see how the leg moves if I—

Elizabeth gasps.

ELIZABETH: But how? Can you do it again? Let me try.

Elizabeth makes the cat's leg move. She gasps, then laughs in delight.

VICTOR: Do you see? Animation after death.

ELIZABETH: But it's only a puppet animated by it's master,
                Victor.

VICTOR: Well, yes. For now. But this is just the beginning.
                There is a great mystery here crying out for me to
                come and discover it.

ELIZABETH: Of course there is. Isn't there always? Speaking of
                mysteries, have you read Spiegel?

Elizabeth pulls a book from the shelf, opens it, and points to a passage.

ELIZABETH: He proposes that if one could limit the quanti-
                ties of certain motes of life, "bacteria" he calls
                them, it might be possible to stop the spread of
                all manner of disease.

VICTOR: But he does not go far enough! None of them do.
                They seek only to prevent disease when instead
                they should encourage the blossom of life itself.

*Elizabeth looks over Victor's chalkboard full of diagrams and then
picks up his journal and begins to read it.*

ELIZABETH: Well I do like the sound of that. Is this one of
                your new studies?

VICTOR: Yes, but it remains unfinished. Pay no attention
                to that. I have yet to solve the problem of—

                (exasperated) A cat, Elizabeth! I busy myself with
                a stray cat when I am on the verge of—

                Ask yourself, whence does the principle of life
                proceed?

ELIZABETH: I have asked it. Many times, and no one has given
                any convincing proof on the matter, as you well
                know.

VICTOR: And whither does life flee at death?

ELIZABETH: A subject upon which any pastor will gladly
                pontificate. Have you joined a seminary in your
                spare time, Victor?

VICTOR: What? This is no inquiry of theology, Elizabeth.
                These are real questions of matter and causation.

ELIZABETH: You have always been passionate for the
                mechanics of the world, Victor. But surely the
                mysteries of Life and Death are not mere matter
                to be manipulated. Perhaps morality ought to
                have a word on the subject.

                Besides, you are not the only one in possession of
                mysteries.

VICTOR: What?

ELIZABETH: A woman also may be a glorious discovery--if
                cowardice does not restrain you.

VICTOR: It is improper to speak so. And I cannot be
               dissuaded from my present studies.

ELIZABETH: Well. That is exactly what a woman wants to
               hear.

               Will you come to dinner tonight?

VICTOR: Dinner? No. Ask Justine to bring something
               later. I shall work a while longer.

ELIZABETH: Later. Always later. Very well.

Elizabeth sighs and exits. Victor considers the cat on his table.

VICTOR: Forgive me, Elizabeth, but my work cannot be
               constrained to cats.

Victor fetches a shovel and looks into the distance.

VICTOR: I must chase the secret of life to its utter end.

*Laughter from the Monster as the scene changes back to the ship.
The Monster (hooded) approaches the stage from the back of the theater and boards the ship. The sailors shout in alarm.*

THE MONSTER: And so does the great man take up the tool of his
             iniquity.

CAPTAIN WINTHROP: Who are you?

THE MONSTER: Tell him, Frankenstein. Confess yourself.

CAPTAIN WINTHROP: Is this one of your men?

THE MONSTER: Hah! You are more right than you can know.

CAPTAIN WINTHROP: Are there others?

The Monster laughs.

VICTOR: So at last you dare to face me?

THE MONSTER: I dare nothing. You are the cause. I am the effect. The rest is destiny.

CAPTAIN WINTHROP: You have a strange manner, sir, and I do not care for it. This is my ship. None trespass here without my leave.

VICTOR: Keep away. Do not approach him. Attend me and all will be made clear.

The Monster sits patiently on the rail of the ship.

THE MONSTER: Do as he says. Attend him.

                  Finish confessing your tale. I will testify to its truth.

The scene changes to a graveyard where Victor works at exhuming a body.

VICTOR: A graveyard was merely a receptacle of raw material for my work. Its secrets I opened...and took.

Victor drags a body to an operating table and begins to experiment upon it.

VICTOR: I saw the form of man degraded and wasted. I saw the worm inherit the wonders of the eye and the brain. I examined all the minutiae of causation seen in the change from life to death, and death to life, until—

Victor staggers back from the operating table as it glows with light.

Victor: —from the midst of darkness illumination
                 dawned. So simple. So clear. I discovered the
                 cause and engine of life!

Upon the operating table an arm slowly rises.

SCENE 3

Alphonse enters.

ALPHONSE: Victor?

VICTOR: Father, come in.

William enters and hugs Victor as Victor hurriedly covers his work.

WILLIAM: Victor!

VICTOR: Hello, little brother.

ALPHONSE: I hope we're not disturbing you.

VICTOR: No, not at all.

WILLIAM: We're going to the watchmaker's shop.

VICTOR: Oh, are you?

ALPHONSE: This accursed old thing can scarcely tell time twice a day, and it will cost a fortune to repair. Sometimes I think the whole course of my life is governed by the infernal creation.

WILLIAM: He says I may have one with my name on it for my birthday.

ALPHONSE: That's not for nearly a month yet, and you still
                have to learn to read time and keep it. We shall
                see.

WILLIAM: Do you want to come with us?

VICTOR: Oh, well, I don't know if—

ALPHONSE: You've been absent lately, and William misses
                you.

VICTOR: Forgive me, little brother. My studies have
                required too much of me.

WILLIAM: What are you working on?

VICTOR: Oh, nothing vitally important. Leave that be.

Justine enters.

JUSTINE: William? There you are. Good morning, sir. I
                apologize. I've been looking everywhere for him.
                Every time I turn around he's run out of sight.

ALPHONSE: It's no harm done. We were just checking in on
                Victor. Take William and get his coat onto him.
                I'll be along shortly.

JUSTINE: Come with me, William. Now.

ALPHONSE: Say goodbye to your brother.

William runs out excitedly.

JUSTINE: That boy. William?!

Justine exits. Alphonse looks around Victor's laboratory.

ALPHONSE: It is not well that a man should be so consumed
                in his work.

VICTOR: Isn't this what you always wanted? For me to
                 find a place and a purpose in the world?

ALPHONSE: Want I wanted? We have not seen you at meals
                 in a fortnight. Your place at the table sits cold
                 and empty.

VICTOR: I'm sorry, Father, but my labors are just. You will
                 see. I will exalt the name of Frankenstein and add
                 it to the company of Newton, DaVinci, Coper-
                 nicus.

ALPHONSE: I, too, was once a man of ambition and power.

VICTOR: I know, Father. You are beloved by everyone I
                 meet.

ALPHONSE: I am told there is now a statue of me in some gray
                 hall of government.

VICTOR: A great honor.

ALPHONSE: And a terrible likeness, I expect.

                 I would trade it all if it would bring her back—

*Alphonse looks up at a portrait of Caroline that looms over Victor's
laboratory.*

VICTOR: I know.

ALPHONSE: —if I could have but one more hour with her.

                 What good did any of it do? The years have
                 slipped away, and what do I have in her place? A
                 cold statue in a dark corner to honor my name.

VICTOR: But she would be proud of you, isn't that what
                 you want?

ALPHONSE: It's not her pride I covet. It's her. You cannot understand.

VICTOR: I do understand. I miss her too.

ALPHONSE: Then what about Elizabeth?

VICTOR: Elizabeth?

ALPHONSE: She has been like a cousin to you, but your cousin she is not. There is affection between you. I have seen it.

VICTOR: Perhaps in a year or two, once I've published my discoveries and...

ALPHONSE: Marriage is a suit best fitted young, while children may yet be the fruit of it.

VICTOR: Children? Father, I—

ALPHONSE: She will be a magnificent bride. Do not forsake her for titles—or statues.

VICTOR: Of course, Father. I will consider it.

ALPHONSE: It's what your *mother* would have wanted, anyway.

Alphonse exits.

Victor returns to his table, uncovering the experiment.

VICTOR: When I found so astonishing a power within my hands, I eagerly considered the best manner in which to employ it.

Victor furiously draws diagrams on a chalkboard and writes in his journal. Victor looks at the portrait of Caroline looming over the laboratory.

VICTOR: The answer was clear. What higher calling could
               there be than to create a beautiful and rational
               being like myself?

*As Victor talks he rushes about gathering body parts and arcane
instruments.*

VICTOR: A new species would bless me as its creator. Many
               lovely and excellent natures would owe their
               being to me. No father could claim the gratitude
               of his children so completely as I should deserve
               theirs.

Victor hacks and sews, doing all sorts of hideous work at his table.

VICTOR: Week after week, I worked in solitude, until at
               last I brought my work near to a conclusion.

SCENE 4

Elizabeth enters. Victor is working slavishly at the table.

ELIZABETH: Victor? What are you doing here?

VICTOR: What?

ELIZABETH: Your brother will be heartbroken if you miss his birthday dinner.

VICTOR: His birthday? Ah. I am sorry, Elizabeth, but I am close! I am so very close!

ELIZABETH: Close to what, Victor? What is this work?

VICTOR: Elizabeth, listen to me. I have done it.

ELIZABETH: Done what?

VICTOR: Life's secrets are open to me. I can draw it forth from that which is dead. I--

ELIZABETH: What dead thing is this?

VICTOR: This? This is my work. It will raise my name to the stars. People will speak of Frankenstein as they do Prometheus!

ELIZABETH: I do not care for your manner, Victor. You do
               not eat. You do not sleep.

VICTOR: Yes, forgive me, but—

ELIZABETH: You have abandoned our companionship—

VICTOR: I have not abandoned you. I only need to finish—

Elizabeth picks up Victor's journal.

ELIZABETH: If this course of study has weakened your affec-
               tions and destroyed your taste for pleasure, then
               this study is unlawful, Victor. It does not befit
               the human mind.

VICTOR: Give me time, Elizabeth. Only a little more. You
               shall be proud of your Victor.

Victor takes the journal and places it in his coat pocket.

ELIZABETH: I will have no Victor left if this passion continues
               to consume him.

VICTOR: I am *right* here. Elizabeth, please.

ELIZABETH: I trust you, for I know your heart. I am jealous
               of it. I will not share it with any other—whether
               womankind or passions of discovery.

VICTOR: Tell William I will attend him as soon I have
               finished. We will be a family as we always have.

ELIZABETH: Good. Then I will look for you at dinner.

*Elizabeth departs. Victor watches her go, then he darkens and turns
to his labors.*

VICTOR: Now let us to it!

Victor removes his coat and hangs it. He builds his creation out of limbs and bloody parts, then attaches to the Monster an apparatus of wires and tubes. Something on the table begins to glow as before.

VICTOR: I say: "Let there be LIFE!"

Victor raises a glowing vial above his head and then plunges it into the heart of the Monster.

VICTOR: And there *was* life.

Victor stares at the Monster.

VICTOR: A wrecked creature, fashioned of gore and bone and withered flesh, but—

The Monster opens his eyes and looks at Victor.

VICTOR: The eyes. Great God!

Victor and the Monster consider one another: Victor with growing horror; the Monster with fear or amazement.

VICTOR: What lurked behind those eyes was a mind, a creature not content merely to be looked upon. No. These eyes looked back!

               And I could not bear their unholy contemplation.

The Monster reaches out to Victor. Victor recoils, then picks up his shovel and strikes the Monster, who falls back to the table seemingly dead. Victor detaches the apparatus and backs out of the room.

VICTOR: My intellect and my curiosity had conspired against me. In their co-mingled fervor they bodied forth a terror unforeseen. If others learned the nature of my work, my name would be consigned to infamy.

All exit.

SCENE 5

The dining room. Alphonse and William are seated at the table. William has his hands over his eyes.

ALPHONSE: Wait. Wait ...

WILLIAM: What is it? Can I look?

ALPHONSE: Not yet. A moment longer ...

Justine enters with a desert on a plate.

JUSTINE: Hide your eyes.

ALPHONSE: Good, good ... and now!

William uncovers his eyes.

WILLIAM: Apple strudel!

JUSTINE: Your favorite. Happy birthday, William!

ALPHONSE: Happy Birthday, son. Now look here.

Alphonse hands William a small box. William opens it and pulls out a pocketwatch.

WILLIAM: A watch!

ALPHONSE: One of your very own. Now you must remember to care for it and keep it wound and keep it always with you. And look here. Your name, as I promised.

WILLIAM: Thank you, Father.

William and Alphonse embrace. Elizabeth enters.

ELIZABETH: Have I missed it?

ALPHONSE: Only just.

ELIZABETH: Happy birthday, William.

ALPHONSE: Victor?

WILLIAM: Is Victor coming?

Elizabeth shakes her head.

ELIZABETH: He is . . . otherwise engaged.

ALPHONSE: Engaged! Will he be wedded to his work as well?

ELIZABETH: He tells me he will join us as soon as he is able.

ALPHONSE: Justine, you know what to do. Save him a portion. Take it to him later.

JUSTINE: Yes, sir.

WILLIAM: I'm going to show Victor my watch!

ALPHONSE: No! Sit.

ELIZABETH: Uncle, please.

ALPHONSE: I have one son apart from my table already. I will not lose the other. Sit, William. And eat. Your brother will come or not.

WILLIAM: Yes, sir.

ELIZABETH: Some strudel for us, Justine, if you will. Would
                you like some, Uncle?

ALPHONSE: What? No. Perhaps later. I have had my fill.
                William may have mine.

JUSTINE: Yes, sir.

Victor stumbles onstage, disheveled.

WILLIAM: Victor! Look what Father gave me!

ALPHONSE: Behold, the prodigal returns at last.

ELIZABETH: Victor, are you well?

VICTOR: Yes. Yes. All is well.

ALPHONSE: He looks ill. Justine bring him a hot tea, and his
                dinner.

Justine exits. Victor sits.

ELIZABETH: What's wrong, Victor?

VICTOR: Wrong? Nothing. Nothing.

ELIZABETH: Have you anything to say to William?

VICTOR: What? Yes. Happy birthday, little brother.

ELIZABETH: Have you completed your work then?

VICTOR: I have. I've put it behind me.

ELIZABETH: And were you successful?

VICTOR: I think I shall change my course of study.

ALPHONSE: Then I will rejoice that I have my family once
                 more. Elizabeth, attend him until he is himself.
                 He needs rest, and a good deal of it.

VICTOR: Forgive me. I've spent these last months in a
                 blind passion. I see now I was misguided.

Justine enters.

JUSTINE: Here you are, sir. Kept rare, just the way you like
                 it.

*Justine sets food down in front of Victor. It is a large leg of mutton
and looks like something from his operating table. Victor wretches.*

ELIZABETH: Victor!

VICTOR: Forgive me. I feel ill. A little rest perhaps.

Victor stumbles out.

THE MONSTER: *(off stage)* Yes, rest! Rest from the work you have
                 cursed and called unholy.

*Transition to the laboratory. Victor enters and stares in horror at
his now empty operating table.*

VICTOR: Oh God. What have I done.

A knock at the door.

ELIZABETH: Victor?

VICTOR: Elizabeth, wait! Do not enter here!

Elizabeth enters.

ELIZABETH: Victor? What are you doing? Are you all right?

Victor is panicked, afraid the Monster is lurking around some corner.

VICTOR: What? Yes. I feel much better.

Elizabeth feels his forehead and examines him.

ELIZABETH: Calm down, Victor. Your heart is racing. Breathe.
                Talk with me. I miss our conversations.

VICTOR: As do I.

Victor searches the room.

ELIZABETH: There are a number of books upon which I intend
                to question you now that you are finished with
                your studies. I may even try my hand at writing
                one myself, perhaps about your work. What do
                you think of that?

                Victor? Victor, what are you doing?

Victor inspects each corner of the room, looking for the Monster.

VICTOR: Doing? Nothing. Only looking for...for some-
                thing I fear I've misplaced.

ELIZABETH: What is it? I will help you find it.

VICTOR: No!

ELIZABETH: What, for God's sake, is the matter? What is the
                cause of all this?

VICTOR: *(pleading)* Do not ask me!

ELIZABETH: My dearest friend is plainly ill and I should not
                ask?

*Elizabeth wanders about the room looking at the wreck. Victor hur-
ries ahead of her, checking around each corner.*

ELIZABETH: Should I not ask after the ghastly wreck of his
                rooms? Should I not question the evidence of
                awful experiments spattered across his table?
                Tell me, Victor. Of which of these should I not
                ask?

VICTOR: Did you not profess your trust in me?

ELIZABETH: I did. But I begin to fear it is some other Victor
                to whom I made the confession.

VICTOR: I am your Victor. I will study subjects more
                mundane, something more suitable to a
                gentlemen. Will you still have me?

ELIZABETH: I would not lose you.

VICTOR: Then let us close up this place. It bears only
                unhappy memories. I will shut it up, and never-
                more darken its door.

                Come. Please.

*Victor boards up the door to the laboratory. Elizabeth exits. When
Victor turns away from the door, he is once again on the icy deck of
the ship.*

SCENE 6

The deck of the ship. The Captain enters.

CAPTAIN WINTHROP: A strange account indeed. But what became of . . . it?

VICTOR: It would have been better had I never again opened that infernal door. But alas, the tale is not yet ended. My woe is scarcely begun.

The Monster enters.

THE MONSTER: Your woe? *(laughs)* A woeful story of a rich young aristocrat and his ill fortune. Is that the flavor of this sorry tale? What of MY woe! Let him hear of THAT!

VICTOR: Heed him not. He is swollen with wrath.

THE MONSTER: And if I am, then who has made me so? TELL Them!

VICTOR: I will tell them of your deeds that they may know what is in your heart.

THE MONSTER: The truth you tell is but half-told. Sit! This tale is MINE now, and I will tell it aright.

CAPTAIN WINTHROP: Then speak! What is your part in this? And what has put such enmity between you and this good man?

VICTOR: Mind your ears. He is eloquent and persuasive. He lies.

THE MONSTER: ENOUGH! Chain your tongue, or I will master it myself—in ways you like not to think.

I alone can tell my tale. And I will tell it. Therefore listen, I command you. All of you. Hear you the true account of Frankenstein and his wicked progeny.

The Monster uncloaks.

CAPTAIN WINTHROP: Great god!

Darkness swallows the stage.

THE MONSTER: To tell how life began is hard, for in the beginning, I was nothing. Darkness hovered over my face.

The scene transitions to Frankenstein's laboratory.

VICTOR: Let there be LIFE!

The lights come up as the Monster awakens on the table.

THE MONSTER: Light poured in upon me.

The Monster and Victor consider one another in fascination.

THE MONSTER: I knew not what who I was or what I was or from what cause. I waked into the world alone and saw about me the shapes of nameless things.

I felt the desire to reach out to another, to one who might sate my need for knowledge and offer a kindly touch, another in whom such life was also lit and—there he stood: my creator.

The Monster reaches out to embrace Victor, but Victor strikes the Monster with the shovel and exits. The Monster stirs. The heartbeat grows.

THE MONSTER: So I had the first of my lessons in the Brotherhood of Man.

VICTOR: *(side stage)* He would have throttled me! I struck only in my defense.

THE MONSTER: I looked for an embrace! And had only violence for an answer. Pain invaded me. Fear sprung up within me! I stumbled in agony through the domain of my waking, taking note of all I saw and all I felt and heard and smelt.

The Monster pulls on Victor's coat containing his journal.

THE MONSTER: But if any fact about my state I knew, 'twas this: I was alone.

And so I fled.

The scene changes to the the street.

THE MONSTER: The city saw me, and hated me.

The Monster flees through the streets. A woman sees him and screams. He runs. He approaches a group of men who beat him. He crawls and is spat upon, laughed at, mocked, and further beaten. The scene transitions to the forest.

THE MONSTER: I ran to the wild. And I ached with loneliness, for

I saw that the birds were not alone, and neither the fish, nor the deer.

The Monster picks a flower and puts it in his coat.

THE MONSTER:Jealously I coveted their company and despaired until—

The Monster sees Agatha with a pail of water. The Monster hides and watches. She is met by a Felix, who is gathering firewood. The Monster follows them to a cottage and observes as they speak with one another and care for De Lacey and an infant, Saffie. As the family converses, the Monster repeats the occasional word or name as he learns to speak.

AGATHA: Come, Papa. Have something to eat.

THE MONSTER: . . . eat . .

DE LACEY: Thank you, Agatha. Potatoes again?

FELIX: There is little else, I'm afraid.

THE MONSTER: . . . afraid . . .

AGATHA: Have you grown tired of my potatoes?

DE LACEY: I've grown tired. But your potatoes are not to blame. Thank you, dear.

AGATHA: Saffie is awake. Was she any trouble, Papa?

THE MONSTER: . . . trouble . . .

DE LACEY: Of course not.

FELIX: Shall I play a song?

AGATHA: Oh, yes! She loves it when you play. But something happy, Felix.

THE MONSTER: . . . happy . . .

FELIX: *(laughs)* Something happy then. Whatever my
                wife commands.

DE LACEY: Are you not going to eat, Felix?

FELIX: I have already eaten, Papa. The rest is for you.

THE MONSTER: . . . Papa . . .

*Felix plays a song as De Lacey eats. Agatha dances playfully and
entertains the child.*

DE LACEY: Will you help me to my bed, Felix?

FELIX: Of course. Sleep well, Papa.

DE LACEY: Play something lonesome. It will settle my mind
                toward sleep.

THE MONSTER: . . . lonesome . . .

FELIX: How about this one?

*Felix plays something slow and mournful. Agatha puts the child
down to sleep.*

AGATHA: Goodnight, Saffie. Goodnight, Papa.

DE LACEY: Goodnight, my dear.

THE MONSTER: . . . goodnight . . .

*They lie down to sleep as Felix plays. The lights dim in the cottage,
and the Monster walks among them as he speaks, though unseen.*

THE MONSTER: I longed to join them, but I dared not. I remem-
                bered too well the treatment I had already
                suffered at the hands of men.

As the Monster narrates, the cottagers wake and go about their work. Agatha cooks and cleans and tends the child. Felix goes outside and fetches water then loads a wheelbarrow with wood. De Lacey sits in his chair and hums to himself.

THE MONSTER: They rose each morning and cared for one another. But all was not always happy.

De Lacey is taken by a bout of coughing. Agatha tries to help. When his coughing subsides, his handkerchief is spotted with blood.

AGATHA: Oh, Papa.

DE LACEY: I am fine, dear. Only a bit of a cough. Don't mind me.

Agatha steps back, looks at this handkerchief and tries to hold back tears.

THE MONSTER: When tears they shed, I was deeply affected by them. For if such lovely creatures were miserable, it was less strange that I should be wretched also.

AGATHA: Come have some tea, Papa.

Agatha patiently serves De Lacey and then steps away and cries softly.

FELIX: Agatha? What is wrong?

Agatha shakes her head to silence Felix and shows him the handkerchief. Felix comforts her.

THE MONSTER: But in those tears, I learned also of comfort. I dreamed that I too could be worthy of compassion, worthy of the tenderness of others.

The Monster: Perhaps, I thought, we were not so different.

Weeks and months I looked on, and from the shadows I collected an education.

Felix and Agatha wander outside with a stack of books and sit beneath a tree as Felix teaches her to read. The Monster watches.

AGATHA: Will you read to me, Felix.

FELIX: Of course, where were we?

AGATHA: Here.

FELIX: God created man in his image: in the image of God he created him: he created them male and female, and—you try.

AGATHA: God . . . saw . . . all . . . that he had . . . mad . . . made!

FELIX: Yes, good. And then?

AGATHA: . . . and lo, it was . . . very . . . good.

Felix and Agatha continue to read silently as the Monster narrates, then they get up and return to the cottage. A book is left behind.

THE MONSTER: I watched hungrily as he taught her, so that as she learned to speak the words on the pages, I could speak them myself and know their meanings.

I discovered from their books all the culture and commerce of Man, of his wealth and his wars and his family relationships.

THE MONSTER: And yet, no father had watched my infant days.

Felix hushes the child.

THE MONSTER: No mother had blessed me with smiles and caresses.

Agatha takes the child and whispers to it.

THE MONSTER: I had not even a childhood.

THE MONSTER: Who was I? What was I? Again and again, the question recurred, it stalked my dreams. It haunted me.

The Monster slips from his hiding place and excitedly seizes the book left behind.

THE MONSTER: From their books I begged an answer to the shape of my ragged form. And page by page they whispered back.

"Paradise Lost."

I learned of Adam, created with care and delight. A perfect and beautiful creature, beloved of his Creator. In his account I found reflected all the questions I groaned with.

THE MONSTER: But in time I came to understand the nature of the pages I had inherited from my own creator.

The Monster withdraws Victor's journal from the coat pocket.

THE MONSTER: The journal of Victor Frankenstein.

Can you conceive of the horror with which I read of MY making? Therein was writ all the means of my accursed origin, down to the minutest description of my loathsome form.

What arm is this? From what man and of what

deeds? What head is this that bears some stranger's face? What heart beats here? What sin indwells this flesh that is not mine?

Have I a patchwork soul as well? Or did he not \ conceived of that detail?

What am I?

And where is the creature who will love ME?!

The Monster tears the journal apart.

THE MONSTER: Upon that unhappy thought, I devised a plan that would lead either to my redemption or to my ruin.

SCENE 7

The Monster gathers wood which he places by the door of the cottage, and lays atop it a flower. De Lacey enters the cottage and sits by the fire. Felix and Agatha attend him. The Monster stands back and watches.

AGATHA: Come and sit, Papa.

DE LACEY: The cold has crept into my bones. Is Saffie warm enough?

AGATHA: Add another log to the fire, Felix. Will you?

FELIX: Of course.

Felix opens the door of the cottage and finds the firewood. He looks around curiously, then carries the wood inside. He fuels the fire then gives the flower to Agatha.

AGATHA: How lovely!

FELIX: An angel has visited us.

AGATHA: I wonder who it is. I'm sure it's Father Pierre, or someone from the church.

DE LACEY: Father Pierre? Has he come to visit?

FELIX: No, Papa. But we'll see him on Sunday.

AGATHA: Are you warm enough?

DE LACEY: Would you bring me another blanket?

FELIX: We're going to check the potatoes and fetch
                 water. Saffie is asleep and we won't be long. Do
                 you need anything else, Papa?

DE LACEY: Go, go. You pay too much attention to an old
                 man. He has lived this long. He will live until
                 you have seen to the potatoes.

*Agatha kisses De Lacey. She and Felix exit. The Monster knocks at
the door.*

DE LACEY: Who's there? Come in.

The Monster enters.

DE LACEY: Father Pierre?

THE MONSTER: No. I am a traveler in want of rest.

DE LACEY: Come in! Come in!

THE MONSTER: I only want to sit by your fire.

DE LACEY: What warmth I have is yours, friend. I am blind,
                 so forgive me if I cannot cook you anything to
                 eat.

THE MONSTER: I need no food. Only kind words. And warmth.

*The two sit in an awkward silence. The Monster gets up and paces,
picks up a book and puts it down again, picks up the guitar and
thinks better of it, then hovers over the child in fascination.*

DE LACEY: Your voice is strange, but by your accent I take
                 you for a countryman.

THE MONSTER: I was educated by a family in this country, yes.

De Lacey: Who are they? Perhaps they are known to me.

The Monster: They may be. I have no friend on earth, but these lovely people.

De Lacey: Be calm, friend. I hear distress in your voice, but you will meet no ill will here.

The Monster: I look after them. I adore them, yet they have never seen me. I dream of going to them, but I am full of fear.

De Lacey: Men are full of brotherly love when treated kindly. If you have looked to their good, as you say, you need not fear. Take hope, friend.

The Monster: I fear I am detestable to look upon.

De Lacey: What matter are appearances. It is the heart and the deed that declare a man. If your actions are as you say, you have naught to fear.

The Monster: Then why am I overwhelmed with terrors? I tenderly love these friends! I have been in the habit of kindness toward them for for many months, and now—

De Lacey: Tell me where these friends reside. Perhaps I will go to them on your behalf.

From offstage, the voices of Agatha and Felix interrupt.

Felix: Do you need help. Let me carry that.

Agatha: I do not like leaving Saffie and Papa so long.

The Monster's anxiety increases.

The Monster: They are very near this spot.

DE LACEY: I am an old man, but it will afford me great pleasure to be serviceable to a fellow creature. I shall do it. I shall intercede for you and convey your good will.

THE MONSTER: From your lips I have heard the first voice of kindness toward me. How can I thank you? I shall be forever grateful.

The baby begins to cry softly and the Monster bends over it unsure what should be done.

DE LACEY: Come then. Tell me the names of your friends.

FELIX: The cold is bitter. I hope the fire has not gone out.

AGATHA: Saffie will be shivering!

The Monster pauses, unable to speak, then begins to weep.

THE MONSTER: They . . . they are . . .

The door of the cottage swings open and Felix and Agatha enter.

THE MONSTER: You and your family are the friends I speak of. Tell them! Save me! Protect me!

FELIX: Who is this?

AGATHA: Papa?

DE LACEY: This friend is in need of help. Reveal yourself, sir. You have not said your name. Let us minister to you with kindness.

THE MONSTER: My name? I . . . I . . .

The Monster lowers his hood. Agatha screams. The Monster cowers and wails. Agatha takes Saffie and holds her protectively.

DE LACEY: Great God! What has happened!

FELIX: Get out, you monster!

THE MONSTER: No! Tell them! I beg you! Save me!

AGATHA: Papa! Get away from him!

DE LACEY: What is it?

AGATHA: Safie, are you all right? Did he hurt you?

FELIX: It is some demon!

De Lacey lifts his cane in fear and confusion. Felix grabs his musket from the wall and fires. The scene freezes.

THE MONSTER: Is this the reward of benevolence? Is this the brotherly love of man? The just effect of kindness?

VICTOR: *(side stage)* What do you know of benevolence or kindness?

THE MONSTER: I loved them! And what was I offered in return? Only cruel blows and a blast of shot!

VICTOR: Would that his aim had been true.

Captain Winthrop enters.

CAPTAIN WINTHROP: Come now. If he offered them kindness and received this violence, then is he misused. Is your hatred not misplaced?

VICTOR: He persuades you, does he? Guard you then your ears until you have heard the tale entire. Then only may you judge me and not before.

You have told your lies! Now I will tell the truth of your murderous ways.

THE MONSTER: What you know of truth we soon shall see.

The Monster exits.

SCENE 8

The mansion.

VICTOR: For months, we were a picture of happiness, though I was haunted by the memory of what I had made, and at all times saw his hideous face before me.

Justine enters.

JUSTINE: Good morning, sir! Master William has spoken of nothing all day but our trip to the market. Will you and Lady Elizabeth join us?

VICTOR: I fear not, Justine. I have arranged for Elizabeth and I to picnic in the garden later. Would you fetch some fresh fruit while you are in town?

JUSTINE: Of course, sir.

William enters.

WILLIAM: Victor!

VICTOR: Good morning, little brother!

WILLIAM: Are you coming with us?

VICTOR: No, no. You go with Justine—and fetch me a fine red apple if you spot one.

WILLIAM: Did you hear that, Miss Justine? We'll find Victor an apple.

JUSTINE: Are you ready? Where is your coat?

William runs to fetch his coat. Elizabeth enters.

ELIZABETH: Good morning, Justine. Are you off to the market?

JUSTINE: Yes, with Master William. I expect we'll return by mid-afternoon.

WILLIAM: Let's go! Let's go!

William runs offstage.

ELIZABETH: Good luck.

JUSTINE: William? William, wait for me! Wait. That boy will be the end of me!

Justine exits.

VICTOR: Will you walk with me?

ELIZABETH: I will. I will talk with you as well, if you ask it.

VICTOR: When have you ever waited for me to ask?

ELIZABETH: I wait for some things, not for others. I am a mystery, Victor. Yours to discover.

VICTOR: As always, you baffle me.

ELIZABETH: Then all is well, and I am content to wait.

VICTOR: These past months have been precious to me. You know that?

ELIZABETH: I feared we—I—had lost you.

VICTOR: Can you forgive me, Elizabeth?

ELIZABETH: Forgive you? For what?

VICTOR: Can you forgive me if I have done something terrible?

ELIZABETH: If it's the unseemly work you speak of, then yes, all is forgiven. It was distasteful perhaps, but not beyond forgiveness. You are too dramatic, Victor, as always.

VICTOR: If I am dramatic, it is only the symptom. Passion is my disease.

ELIZABETH: And what then is the cure?

VICTOR: *(taking her hand)* I fear I am incurable.

ELIZABETH: I see you are recovered to your true self.

VICTOR: I pray you are right.

ELIZABETH: Be at peace, Victor. All is right in the world. The air is crisp and clear. Your father and brother are happy and hale. The shadows are flown.

VICTOR: There is something I have delayed asking for far too long, and your patience has been a reviving grace.

ELIZABETH: Then delay no longer, Victor. I am here. I will answer.

Victor kneels.

VICTOR: Will you be my wife? Though I scarcely deserve
               to ask it, I do.

ELIZABETH: You know too little what you deserve. Yes. I will
               have you for my husband, and no other.

VICTOR: Oh Elizabeth, I am so full of terrors—but now
               they are mixed with happiness.

A shadow passes across the stage.

VICTOR: Did you see that?

ELIZABETH: See what?

VICTOR: I thought I saw a figure there, upon the edge of
               the forest.

ELIZABETH: See this figure, Victor. See me. I will lay your
               terrors to rest. Now come, we must tell your
               father and his joy will multiply our own.

SCENE 9

The mansion. Alphonse enters.

ELIZABETH: Uncle! Victor and I have something to tell you. We have happy news.

                    What's wrong? Is everything all right?

ALPHONSE: William—

VICTOR: William? He's gone with Justine to the market.

ALPHONSE: He is murdered.

VICTOR: What?

ELIZABETH: That cannot be!

ALPHONSE: Strangled.

ELIZABETH: Strangled?!

ALPHONSE: In the wood at the edge of town.

ELIZABETH: But how? Why?

ALPHONSE: How could my sweet boy provoke such an act!

ELIZABETH: Who would do such a thing.

VICTOR: I fear I know who.

ALPHONSE: The murderer is already found.

VICTOR: He is found? Then thank God!

ALPHONSE: It is Justine.

VICTOR: Justine?

ELIZABETH: There must be some mistake!

ALPHONSE: They say she was crouching over his body like a crone, robbing him of the watch I gave him for his birthday.

VICTOR: Where is she now?

ALPHONSE: They have taken her before the magistrate.

ELIZABETH: Victor you must go to her. Oh God! My poor William!

ALPHONSE: My little boy. I want to see him. I want to see his body. Where is he?

Elizabeth comforts her uncle, weeping with him.

VICTOR: Stay with him. I will see that her innocence is upheld.

Elizabeth and Alphonse exit.

THE MONSTER: *(side stage)* Now we will see something of monsters and murder.

                Tell them, Frankenstein! And let them be the judge of what is monstrous here.

The scene changes to the courtroom. Justine enters with Victor and stands before the Judge.

JUDGE: Order! Order!

We are here to decide the guilt of this woman found in the act of murdering the child, William Frankenstein.

VICTOR: Your honor, if I may speak.

JUDGE: You may.

VICTOR: I have known the accused for many years. She is the faithful governess of my brother who is now murdered.

JUDGE: And do you have evidence to support her innocence?

VICTOR: It is plain that she could not do such a thing. I suspect some evil-hearted wretch has escaped your notice.

JUDGE: Have you evidence of such a wretch?

VICTOR: Evidence? No. But I saw a figure near the wood. Perhaps a search of the area—

JUDGE: Can you describe this figure? Was it man or woman?

VICTOR: I cannot say. But surely if we search—

JUDGE: This court must concern itself with evidence, sir. If you have knowledge of "some evil-hearted wretch" then speak, or else let the engine of justice proceed.

Victor is silent.

JUDGE: Let the accused testify to her actions. What say you?

JUSTINE: I am innocent.

JUDGE: Tell us the way of it.

JUSTINE: I lost sight of William at the market and—

The Monster steps forward to address the audience as the scene in the courtroom freezes.

THE MONSTER: I will tell the way of it. I fled the cottage that had shunned my kindness, and ran with haste to the place I had been made, for to confront my maker and demand of him answers.

WILLIAM: *(offstage)* Apples! This way! We'll pluck a fresh one! Come on!

An apple rolls onto the stage and the Monster picks it up.

THE MONSTER: But here was a child unspoilt by hatred or vanity or greed, and in his innocence perhaps he would look upon me kindly and turn not away.

William enters. The Monster (hooded) approaches William with an apple in his outstretched hand.

WILLIAM: Who are you?

THE MONSTER: Come. Take it. I will not harm you.

WILLIAM: My father says I am not to take gifts from strangers.

THE MONSTER: Then let us not be strangers. We shall be friends. Take it. No harm will come to you. Here.

William approaches the Monster.

WILLIAM: I'm looking for an apple to give to my brother.

THE MONSTER: This is a fine one. You may have it. Is your brother near?

William takes hold of the apple, though the Monster does not release it.

WILLIAM: He's at home. Thank you, sir.

The Monster lowers his hood. William recoils in fright.

THE MONSTER: Wait! Why do you recoil? Take my gift. It is freely given.

WILLIAM: I don't want your apple.

THE MONSTER: You refuse my kindness? Why?

WILLIAM: I don't like you.

THE MONSTER: I am terrible to look upon, but I will not harm you. Wait! Take it! Please.

WILLIAM: When I tell my father about you he will have you arrested!

THE MONSTER: Arrested? I have done nothing but offer you an apple!

WILLIAM: I hate you!

William turns to run. The Monster seizes him and William drops his pocketwatch.

THE MONSTER: What crime have I committed? I have broken no law.

WILLIAM: Give me my watch! Let me go! You're a monster! Don't touch me! Let me go.

THE MONSTER: Quiet!

The Monster picks up the watch and looks at it.

THE MONSTER: William Frankenstein?

WILLIAM: Give it back to me! It's mine!

JUSTINE: William, where are you?

WILLIAM: Let me go! My brother will hate you like I do, he will kill you! Let me go!

THE MONSTER: *Frankenstein.*

JUSTINE: William?

WILLIAM: Help—

The Monster covers William's mouth to quiet him and begins to squeeze him as he struggles to get free.

THE MONSTER: Quiet! QUIET!

William dies and the Monster tries to shake William awake, but hearing Justine's approach, he flees, exiting with William's body. Justine kneels beside the watch in shock. She plucks the watch from the ground. The Courtroom scene resumes.

JUSTINE: —and when I found him, he was dead.

JUDGE: And did you not take from the boy a valuable watch?

JUSTINE: I did, sir. But only because I did not wish it lost.

JUDGE: Bring forth the witnesses to the scene.

The Village Woman and Baker enter.

JUDGE: Speak ye true. Bear witness.

VILLAGE WOMAN: I was on my way home from the bakery up the street when the little master, ran past and nearly knocked me over.

JUDGE: You mean the boy William? The victim?

VILLAGE WOMAN: Yes, sir. I knew him. We all know Mssr. Frankenstein and his family.

                I saw him run away down the street, and I thought how sweet he looked and how like his father, and then the awful woman came. I heard her shout, "I will throttle you!"

JUSTINE: But I only meant that—

JUDGE: Silence! Continue.

VILLAGE WOMAN: You can look at her to see she's an awful sort. A terrible person, I think. She ran around shouting for the boy, and I thought to myself, the boy will be treated badly when she finds him.

JUSTINE: I was worried for him!

VILLAGE WOMAN: Then I heard something from the direction of the forest. Something like an unhappy child. So I told the baker to come with me. The baker told another man, two men, to come. When we got there she had her hands on him and she had murdered the boy. She tried to run away and I cried out "Murder!" and then we took her. The boy was dead. Sweet boy. He looked like an angel.

JUDGE: And you, you are the baker?

BAKER: I am.

JUDGE: And what say you?

BAKER: That is the way of it. She was filching the watch when we found her.

JUDGE: How answer you these accusations?

JUSTINE: I am innocent! I found poor William and—I loved him!

JUDGE: Saw you no one else who might be accused?

JUSTINE: I saw no one. I cannot make sense of it.

JUDGE: Then unless some other can offer evidence of one who may have done this murder, it seems your guilt is sealed.

VICTOR: No!

JUDGE: Have you some knowledge, sir?

VICTOR: It is plain to see that she is guiltless. She is a tender woman with no violence in her.

JUDGE: Even those who appear innocent may harbor monstrous desires. But if you know of some brute who may have struck down this child, speak of it. These good people have given witness, and there is none to gainsay them.

VICTOR: What can I do? I know only that this woman is innocent.

JUDGE: Though she may yet be guiltless, all judges had rather that ten innocent should suffer than one guilty should go free.

JUSTINE: What? No!

JUDGE: Therefore I judge thee guilty of murder, and on the gibbet shall ye hang.

The villagers nod in satisfaction.

VICTOR: *(to the audience)* Did I not tell you he had murder in his heart? Now you know the truth of it. He is a destroyer of innocents! The blood of my brother stains his monstrous hands!

The Monster drags Justine to the gibbet, while the villagers cheer.

THE MONSTER: What's monstrous here is *Man*, who even in a child has instilled hatred toward one who only asked for kindness.

                What's monstrous here is *justice*, which has sacrificed the innocent to its bloodlust!

The crowd cries "Hang her, hang her!" The Monster puts the noose around Justine's neck.

THE MONSTER: What's monstrous here is the *craven heart* that keeps its silence while a guiltless neck is stretched upon the gibbet!

The Monster hoists the rope and Justine is hung. The crowd cheers.

VICTOR: We have heard of your violence from your own tongue. Your sins cannot be shifted.

THE MONSTER: My sins I own, and I have no need to cover them. Can you say the same?

Finish the tale, and then some better judge may tell.

The Monster exits.

SCENE 10

VICTOR: Our grief consumed us. And in my heart I doubled my own tortures, for I had spoken not in Justine's defense.

Victor pleads with Justine's hanging body.

VICTOR: But what might I have said? Should I have confessed to the creation of a hateful brute who ranged the countryside in his bloodlust? Who would have believed it? Had I spoken, I would only have redoubled our grief.

Alphonse and Elizabeth enter and consider Justine's death.

VICTOR: Elizabeth became cold. My father silent. And I fled into the hills to drown my cries in the solitude of nature.

Alphonse and Elizabeth exit.

THE MONSTER: Now shall we pierce to the heart of the tale!

VICTOR: It was there he came to me. I saw him first from afar, bounding from hill to hill with inhuman strength. He approached, nearer and nearer, until with a leap he stood before me in all his wretched fury.

Make ready to defend yourself. For William, my brother, I shall slay thee, and curse the wretched life I gave.

THE MONSTER: All men hate the wretched! Even you, my creator, detest me. Now you purpose to kill me. Come, then! Do your duty, and I will do mine.

Victor and the Monster rush at one another and lock in combat. The Monster easily hurls Victor away.

THE MONSTER: You cannot slay me! But comply with my conditions, and I will leave you in peace.

VICTOR: Conditions? The fiend comes to treat as a man?

THE MONSTER: If you refuse me, I will glut the maw of death and sate it with the blood of all you love.

VICTOR: Come then, that I may extinguish the spark of life I lit!

They fling themselves at one another again. And again the Monster eludes Victor.

THE MONSTER: Look on me, Frankenstein. I am powerful, but I will be mild and docile, if only you will grant that which you owe me.

VICTOR: Owe you? I owe you nothing!

THE MONSTER: I am your creation! I am your Adam! I was benevolent and good, till misery made me a fiend. Believe me, Frankenstein, my being glowed with love and humanity.

VICTOR: My brother is slain, and he too glowed with love till you snuffed it cold. There can be no community between you and me. We are enemies eternal.

THE MONSTER: Yet it is in your power to redeem me. Let your compassion be moved.

VICTOR: What cause have I to visit compassion upon a murderer?

THE MONSTER: Murder? Who was it kept silent while an innocent was hanged? And now you spew the accusation even as you would visit murder upon your own creation.

Oh, praise the eternal justice of Man! Do you not admit your own paradox?

VICTOR: Your mock morality has no claim on me. You speak in circles.

THE MONSTER: LISTEN to me! For on you it rests, whether I quit forever the neighborhood of man or else become the author of your ruin.

VICTOR: Speak then. But do not think your lies will find any root.

THE MONSTER: As Almighty God looked down on Adam and judged his loneliness ill, so I must sway you to judge my own and amend it.

VICTOR: What blasphemy do you imply?

THE MONSTER: Create for me a companion. One with whom I can live in equity and love. This you alone can do.

If any being felt emotions of benevolence toward me, for that one creature's sake I would make peace with all the earth!

VICTOR: You are maddened.

The Monster seizes Victor and begins to throttle him.

THE MONSTER: If I cannot inspire love, I will cause fear, and chiefly in you, my arch-enemy, because on you I swear inextinguishable hatred. I will work at your destruction, and neither will I finish until I desolate your heart.

The Monster looses Victor. Victor staggers back and drops to the floor.

VICTOR: You cannot ask this of me.

THE MONSTER: What I ask of you is just.

VICTOR: And what when she wakes and recoils from your form as all others do? Will you make of her a slave to your base passions?

THE MONSTER: She would not recoil. But if she should, so be it. She will enjoy the choice you withheld from me. And while there is yet another on the earth like myself, I will go forth in hope rather than despair.

VICTOR: You will yet be hated. And she with you.

THE MONSTER: It is true, our lives will not be happy, but they will be harmless and free from the loneliness I now feel.

VICTOR: You cannot understand what you ask.

The Monster drops to his knees and begs.

The Monster: Oh, my creator! Let me feel gratitude toward you for this one blessing! Consent, and you shall never see me again.

Hear my prayer. Grant what I desire.

Victor: You swear to fly from the habitations of Man?

The Monster: We will abandon the world of men forever. My life will flow quietly away, and in my dying moments I shall *bless* my maker's name.

Victor: Then on your oath, I consent.

The Monster: By the sun and by the fire of love in my heart, I do swear it. And when my prayer is answered you will see me no more.

Go in peace, Frankenstein. I shall watch, and when you are ready, I shall appear.

The Monster exits. Captain Winthrop enters.

Captain Winthrop: Great god, man. What have you done?

Victor: May God have mercy on my soul.

Victor enters his laboratory and kneels before his operating table like a bloody altar.

Victor: Stars! Winds! Fates! Take pity! Crush me now and make me nothing. Or else depart and leave me in my darkness, for unto a grim new work I now devote my life.

Victor hurls the cover from the table, raises a meat cleaver and brings it down violently. Darkness envelopes the stage.

ACT II

SCENE 1

The stage is set with a child's coffin. Elizabeth, Alphonse, Victor, and Pastor enter and gather around it. Upstage, a lone gravedigger lowers Justine from the gibbet and drags her body offstage.

PASTOR: As Christ was raised from the dead, we too are called to follow him through death and into glory.

            For Christ is the firstborn of the dead; to him be glory and power forever and ever.

COMPANY: Amen.

PASTOR: You knew me before I was born. You shaped me into your image and likeness.

COMPANY: I breathe forth my spirit to you, my Creator.

PASTOR: Lazarus you raised, O Lord, from the decay of the tomb.

COMPANY: Grant your servant rest.

PASTOR: To you we commend the soul of William your
                servant. In your sight may he live forever. In your
                goodness grant him everlasting life.

COMPANY: Amen.

As the Pastor completes the funeral rite and exits, Elizabeth tries to comfort Alphonse.

ALPHONSE: I ought to have been there. I ought to have
                stopped it. Let go of me. Why didn't someone
                help him! I cannot even keep my own family
                safe!

ELIZABETH: Come, Uncle. William is at peace. We must turn
                our attentions to the living.

ALPHONSE: Thank God his mother didn't live to see this.

VICTOR: We mourned, we buried the dead, and I worked
                at creating the new life I had promised, though I
                did so slowly, for I dreaded its completion.

ALPHONSE: She would be ashamed. I've failed her.

VICTOR: But winter could not withhold spring forever.
                And as the land bloomed and rose from her
                tomb, our spirits blossomed as well.

Elizabeth dries her tears as Alphonse exits dejectedly.

VICTOR: My dear, it warms my heart to see your joy return.

ELIZABETH: Yet your father grows slower each day, Victor.
                Have you not noticed?

VICTOR: When Mother died he invested all his love of her
                in William. I think he had little left for the rest

of us. And now that William is gone—

ELIZABETH: But we have it in our power to grant him a boon, Victor, a blessing that may restore him, or at least grant him happiness in his last years.

VICTOR: What boon?

ELIZABETH: Let us forestall no longer and be married, so he may enjoy the union of those he cherishes most.

VICTOR: You're right. Of course you are. But there's something I must do first, Elizabeth. Something I have put off for too long.

ELIZABETH: What is this thing? Tell me.

VICTOR: I cannot.

ELIZABETH: Are we here again, then? What is it you cannot say to me, Victor? What manner of thing can stand between us, who have kept no secrets ever?

VICTOR: But I have, Elizabeth. God forgive me, but I have kept secrets. And if I do not tend to them they will return to haunt me.

ELIZABETH: Do you remember when we were children, Victor? We shared everything. There was a time when all our secrets were between us and together we kept them from the world. Do not withdraw from me. Let me bear this secret with you.

VICTOR: Forgive me. But what I withhold from you, I withhold for your safety.

ELIZABETH: And what if by keeping me safe, you lose what

you hope to protect.

VICTOR: Trust in your Victor as you once did. I have a task to complete, and later, when it is done, all secrets will be put to death. I swear it!

ELIZABETH: Later. Always later. Very well then, Victor. See to your secrets.

Elizabeth exits.

SCENE 2

Victor enters the laboratory

VICTOR: By day I slept, and by night I crept once more among the dead, heaving out of the earth the raw material of my work.

Victor hauls a body to his table, hacks and hews and sews, sweaty and bloody in his work. The Monster enters and watches.

THE MONSTER: My creator fashioned for me another of my own kind, a companion, that I might not be alone.

I looked on with tears of joy, as piece by piece she was stitched into a being of terrible beauty. To look on her you would pale, but to these eyes her every bone and ligament was as the finest gold.

Each night, I waited and watched for the moment of her wakening.

The Monster steps into shadow. Elizabeth enters and walks quietly around the room, looking at Victor's work.

ELIZABETH: What is this?

VICTOR: Elizabeth! No! Get out!

ELIZABETH: I will not! I want to help you, Victor! Why won't
                  you let me help you?

VICTOR: You cannot! Such work does not befit a woman.

ELIZABETH: How then can it befit a man? Show me.

Elizabeth approaches the laboratory table.

VICTOR: No. Please. Wait!

ELIZABETH: Let me go! Let me see.

VICTOR: Listen to me, Elizabeth. I did it.

ELIZABETH: What did you do?

VICTOR: I can command . . . life—as God above.

ELIZABETH: That is not possible.

VICTOR: But it is, Elizabeth. I have done it.

ELIZABETH: Show me. I want to see.

VICTOR: No! You cannot!

ELIZABETH: And why is that? I'm already here, Victor. Move
                  aside and let me see.

VICTOR: He is . . . he is detestable. He's an abomination
                  unfit for human eyes.

ELIZABETH: Nonsense. If you have given life to the lifeless
                  then you have wrought a thing of beauty, Victor.
                  The appearance of it is a small matter.

VICTOR: He is a murderer, Elizabeth.

ELIZABETH: This? Is this the source of your distress? All I see
                  lies dead upon your table.

VICTOR: Not that. That is another.

ELIZABETH: Another? What do you mean?

VICTOR: He demands it, Elizabeth, and I have sworn it to him.

ELIZABETH: Who demands? What are you talking about? Be sensible and explain it to me. You sound like a madman.

The Monster steps out of the shadows, cloaked.

THE MONSTER: The Lord God said, "It is not good that the man should be alone. I will make for him a helper to be his wife."

VICTOR: Stay back!

Elizabeth is not afraid, but transfixed. The Monster and Elizabeth circle one another in fascination.

ELIZABETH: Can you speak with me?

VICTOR: Elizabeth come away!

Elizabeth waves Victor away.

ELIZABETH: What is your name?

THE MONSTER: My name is his to conjure, for who can name himself. It is his to choose if mine be Hatred or else be Love. And upon his choice hangs the ruin or life of all the neighborhood of Man.

ELIZABETH: Choice? What choice?

VICTOR: I have already agreed to your pact! Begone or I may think of it again and alter my course.

The Monster seizes Elizabeth by the arm.

THE MONSTER: Fulfill your promise. My wedding night awaits me, and with it your absolution.

The Monster pushes Elizabeth toward Victor and vanishes into the shadows.

VICTOR: Are you harmed? Did he hurt you?

ELIZABETH: Harmed? I am entranced. You made this being? Its life is from your hands?

VICTOR: I confess it. I knew not what I did, and I would unmake it if I could. Can you forgive me?

ELIZABETH: Forgive you? Victor, this is a miracle.

VICTOR: A miracle?

ELIZABETH: You have done what only God may do. I know not whether it is blasphemy or some high art, but it is unparalleled in the science of Man. And now you are making another? A woman?

VICTOR: He demands it of me. If I withhold from him a companion, he will desolate the earth. He is powerful, Elizabeth. And his heart is black.

ELIZABETH: The creature I just beheld was not black of heart. He spoke as a soul bereft of human love. I heard in his voice an echo of my own, Victor, for who has not known the despair of loneliness and cried out to her maker for its amendment?

VICTOR: Elizabeth, do not be swayed. He has no kindness in him, and he is murderous.

ELIZABETH: What murder has he done?

VICTOR: William.

ELIZABETH: What did you say?

VICTOR: He slew William in his rage. And Justine has
              hung for it.

ELIZABETH: That cannot be.

VICTOR: It is. I swear it.

ELIZABETH: But that's impossible, Victor. How—

VICTOR: Must I defend my word against an abomination?

ELIZABETH: If this is so then why did you not speak of it?

VICTOR: I tried!

ELIZABETH: You tried?

VICTOR: What was I to say? Should I have confessed that I
              delved in graveyards like a heretic and fashioned
              a creature out of the freshly dead?

              Should I have told them that I gave a brute the
              gift of life and in return it gorged its evil upon an
              innocent's blood?

              My name would have been mocked for a
              madman's. And yet would Justine *still have hung.*

ELIZABETH: Yet you told not even me, Victor!

VICTOR: Is it not the burden of prudence to keep silent?

ELIZABETH: Prudence!?

VICTOR: For your sake, Elizabeth! For your sake!

ELIZABETH: You suggest that a woman has hanged for my sake, and I ought to thank you for it? Oh God! Poor Justine!

VICTOR: You do not understand. You cannot.

ELIZABETH: You are right, Victor. I do not understand.

             You tell me you have sinned in the making of this creature, but to have abandoned Justine? To know the truth and keep it for yourself? Such silence broods a cold and cruel iniquity, Victor, and I am ashamed to see it rooted in the man I am to wed.

VICTOR: I had no choice, Elizabeth.

ELIZABETH: At every turn you push me away. You drive me out. You close yourself off. You sequester yourself with corpses rather than share your passion with the beating heart of one loves you.

VICTOR: Elizabeth, please, I—

ELIZABETH: You must love in return, Victor.

VICTOR: I do, Elizabeth. I do.

ELIZABETH: I have been a fool. Perhaps it is fitting that I am to wed a fool as well. For your father's tender heart I will not break our betrothal. But be you sure that when you visit me upon our wedding night, it will be a cold bed that greets you.

VICTOR: Elizabeth, please. I should have confided in you. I should have—

ELIZABETH: If there is to be forgiveness, it will come in some distant time that I cannot yet see.

Goodbye, Victor. Dabble with your miracles. I will see you when we are wed.

Elizabeth exits.

VICTOR: Elizabeth!

Victor turns on the nearly finished Bride on the table.

VICTOR: Accursed work! Surely I am wedded to misery.

The Monster's voice answers from the shadows.

THE MONSTER: Finish your work, Frankenstein, and I will quit you forever.

VICTOR: Then let us to it!

Victor goes to work at the table. As he does so, Alphonse and Elizabeth make wedding preparations. As Elizabeth is made ready, so is the Bride.

ALPHONSE: The wedding will be in the old church. It is the very place I was wed and my parents before me.

ELIZABETH: Yes, Uncle.

ALPHONSE: You must call me "father" now, and I shall call you "daughter." The days are few before it shall be lawfully so.

ELIZABETH: Yes, Father.

ALPHONSE: We must summon the dressmaker. I will spare no expense.

ELIZABETH: Yes, Father.

The Dressmaker enters.

ALPHONSE: Sew for her a gown of purest white. My Eliza-
                 beth will be made to shine like a jewel.

DRESSMAKER: It shall be my finest work.

ALPHONSE: You must be exquisite.

ELIZABETH: Yes, Father.

The Dressmaker exits. The Pastor enters.

PASTOR: At the appointed time, the bride and groom
                 will process to the altar here. The vows shall be
                 spoken and the marriage consecrated.

ALPHONSE: Do you understand, my dear?

ELIZABETH: Yes, Father.

ALPHONSE: Tomorrow will be a day of great joy! You have
                 made me a happy man, my dear. We will make of
                 you a true Frankenstein.

ELIZABETH: Yes, Father.

*Alphonse and Elizabeth exit. Victor finishes his work, attaches the
apparatus to the Bride, and then raises the glowing vial.*

VICTOR: I raise thee a bride to rid the world of the curse I
                 have loosed upon it.

The Monster enters.

THE MONSTER: Flesh like my flesh.

*Victor steps back, the glowing vial still in his hand. The Monster
approaches the table.*

THE MONSTER: Yours shall be all the love and care that was
denied me. You shall be beloved. The wild
reaches of creation shall be our home. And we
will live and love and bear children as all things
do. Man shall neither think on us nor trouble us
any longer.

Finish your work, Frankenstein. Fulfill your
covenant.

VICTOR: Let there be—

Children? Said you nothing of children.

THE MONSTER: What of it? If any offspring come of our union,
they will be no concern of yours or any man.

VICTOR: Will God forgive me if I am cause for the creation
of a race of devils?

THE MONSTER: Wake her.

VICTOR: What right have I to inflict such a curse upon
everlasting generations?

THE MONSTER: Waken her!

VICTOR: Future ages will curse me, whose work imperiled
the whole human race.

THE MONSTER: WAKEN her!

VICTOR: The name of Frankenstein cannot be recalled in
infamy! You ask too much!

Victor smashes the vial on the floor. The light is extinguished.

THE MONSTER: NOOO!! Do you dare break your oath? Will
you make of me your Satan rather than your

Adam?

VICTOR: I do break my promise. Never will I create another like yourself.

THE MONSTER: Have you forgotten what power I possess?! What strength? You are my creator, but I am your master now. OBEY!

VICTOR: The hour of my irresolution is past. I am inexorable.

The Monster hurls Victor away and crawls on the floor, trying to gather up the pieces of the vial and make them glow. He rattles the apparatus attached to the Bride, trying to discern its workings. He shakes her, he breaths into her mouth. He raises her up and embraces her.

THE MONSTER: Nooo! Wake her! Call her to life! I *command* it!

VICTOR: I have declared to you my intent. My labors are finished.

The Monster sobs over the Bride.

THE MONSTER: Then teach me the manner of your work! I will do it! Do not send me into the world alone! You MADE ME, but made me only in half! Complete the work you began!

Victor exits. The Monster weeps over the Bride and then gathers her up in his arms.

THE MONSTER: We are NOT finished, Frankenstein. We are not FINISHED!

The Monster exits carrying the Bride and weeping.

SCENE 3

Wedding music. The church. Elizabeth and Alphonse process onto the stage and meet Victor standing before the altar (which mirrors the operating table from the last scene).

PASTOR: O God, who in creating the human race willed that man and wife should be one, join these in the covenant of Marriage, so that they may become witnesses to charity itself.

COMPANY: Amen.

PASTOR: Who gives this woman to be wed to this man.

ALPHONSE: As God gave Eve to Adam, so do I give Elizabeth to Victor.

VICTOR: I, Victor, take you, Elizabeth, for my wife, to have and to hold, to love and to cherish until death do us part.

ELIZABETH: I, Elizabeth, take you, Victor, for my husband, to have and to hold, to love and to cherish until death do us part.

PASTOR: May you be witnesses in the world to God's

charity, so that the afflicted and needy who have known your kindness may one day receive you into the eternal dwelling of God.

COMPANY: Amen.

PASTOR: What God has put together, let no man put asunder. Go forth in the name of the Lord.

All exit.

SCENE 4

Victor carries Elizabeth into the wedding bower.

VICTOR: Elizabeth?

Elizabeth ignores Victor.

VICTOR: Elizabeth . . . I—

ELIZABETH: Do not speak. Let no words disturb us now.

VICTOR: Am I forgiven?

ELIZABETH: To forgive is a journey. Today is but a step.

VICTOR: Then I have yet hope.

ELIZABETH: I cannot hate you, my Victor. My husband. So let us begin, tonight, to create a new love from what has died. Death unto rebirth is the way of all life. It will be our way as well.

VICTOR: There is nothing hidden between us. I will be a new man, Elizabeth, your creation.

A shadow passes. Victor pushes Elizabeth away and looks wildly around the room.

VICTOR: He cannot enter!

ELIZABETH: What?

Victor goes to the door and looks out. He closes it. Locks it. Ensures its security.

ELIZABETH: There is no one here, Victor, only you and I.

Faint laughter.

VICTOR: NO!

ELIZABETH: Victor!

Victor rushes to the dresser and withdraws a pistol. He runs to the window, the door, waving the pistol madly.

VICTOR: Get away!

ELIZABETH: Victor what is this!

VICTOR: He stalks me, Elizabeth. Did you hear him? Did you see his shadow passing? These are my secrets in the flesh.

ELIZABETH: I heard only the wind on the window, saw only a flash of firelight on the curtain. There is no trouble here.

VICTOR: I want to believe you. But you cannot know how he hates me. I live ever in the foreshadow of his appearance.

ELIZABETH: Be at peace, Victor. Love alone can quiet terror. Mine shall conquer yours.

Victor falls to his knees and Elizabeth comforts him.

ELIZABETH: Did you fulfill your promise to him?

VICTOR: I could not. And now I fear him as never before.

As Elizabeth talks, the Monster emerges from the shadows behind her.

ELIZABETH: Listen to me. You are my husband. I am your
                  wife. We will kindle a new life between us. We
                  shall be blessed with children to love and cherish
                  and train up in kindness and knowledge.

                  We will withdraw to the country and—

THE MONSTER: No.

Elizabeth screams. Victor raises the gun.

VICTOR: Away, devil! Do not threaten what is dearest me.
                  You will rue it.

THE MONSTER: You would take for yourself that which you deny
                  me?

VICTOR: My oath I have broken, I confess it. For no oath
                  can be held between a man and an abomination.

THE MONSTER: You dissemble. The god you worship bound
                  himself to a covenant with your kind, even unto
                  his own death.

                  Are you not made in his image?

VICTOR: I will not hear you! You have no right to speak of
                  gods and men.

THE MONSTER: Were your god to you as you have been to me,
                  only his ruin would slake your hatred. Who then
                  am I to rise higher than my maker?

VICTOR: You delight to talk as if you look down upon me from a righteous throne. But you are not my judge. I made you. I stitched you out of better men and the best of you is no more than the tatters they left behind.

THE MONSTER: Then tell me why, Frankenstein. Why did you make me? Not to love. Not to cherish. But to torment? To hate? Why, Frankenstein. Why!?

VICTOR: I owe you no defense.

ELIZABETH: Victor, put the pistol down.

THE MONSTER: What seed was planted that germinated within you? What grub of the mind grew and enfleshed itself in my patchwork form?

VICTOR: You are a child of science, nothing more. Nothing more!
(to the audience/Captain)
His inquisitions pierced me. They plumbed my soul, and even as he asked it, I felt that his soundings had divined some hidden shape within me, some primal cause of which I was merely the effect and destined result.

Alphonse enters.

VICTOR: Father!?

ALPHONSE: He's awake! I think he wants his mother. Caroline?

A shadowed figure, Caroline, enters and uncloaks.

CAROLINE: My son.

VICTOR: Mother?

CAROLINE: Look at him. Look at his eyes! He sees me! How
               lovely. Such intelligence!

ALPHONSE: What a magnificent thing we have made.

CAROLINE: He is our creation, whom to bring up to good,
               and whose lot it is in our hands to direct toward
               happiness.

VICTOR: My mother—a creature of absolute grace and
               charity.

CAROLINE: Victor? Victor, come and see.

ALPHONSE: A surprise for you.

CAROLINE: She will be with us now. Not a sister exactly but a
               cousin perhaps. A companion for you. We must
               make her happy, Victor.

ALPHONSE: She is bereaved of her family, therefore we shall
               be hers in all ways and love her like our own.

CAROLINE: Come, child. Tell him your name. Let us minister
               to you with kindness.

Victor tenderly lifts her chin. She smiles. Caroline and Alphonse exit.

ELIZABETH: I am Elizabeth.

*A bed rolls onstage. Caroline lies on it and cries out as Alphonse
delivers William. The sheets are soaked with blood.*

ALPHONSE: Another boy! He is beautiful!

CAROLINE: Victor! Come. Quickly. Listen to me.

VICTOR: Are you well, Mother? What's wrong?

CAROLINE: I must leave you, I fear.

VICTOR: What?

CAROLINE: Care for them, Victor. For Elizabeth. For your
                 father. For little William. You will make me
                 proud, won't you?

VICTOR: Where are you going? What do you mean?
                 When are you coming back?

CAROLINE: You are a Frankenstein, Victor. Remember that.
                 Make me proud. Make me proud.

ALPHONSE: What's going on? What did she say? Caroline?
                 Caroline!

*Victor steps back in growing horror as Caroline and the bed are
rolled away into darkness.*

VICTOR: Mother!

ALPHONSE: Caroline!

*The baby cries as the bed is replaced with a coffin around which the
family weeps as a Pastor performs a funeral rite.*

Victor falls to his knees.

PASTOR: All who have died in Christ, will rise with him
                 on the last day. We give you thanks, O Lord. You
                 are the resurrection and the life. Amen.

ALPHONSE: Hush, little William. She is gone to God. Hush,
                 my son.

The Pastor exits with the coffin.

ALPHONSE: Would that we had done something more for
                 her. Now we shall dwell always in the shadow of
                 her passing.

Alphonse exits. Caroline crosses the stage and whispers in his ear.

CAROLINE: You are a *Frankenstein.*

Caroline exits.

THE MONSTER: Answer me. Why was I made, and to what end?

VICTOR: My reasons are my own. They are no concern of
                 yours.

THE MONSTER: No concern? They are my chief and only
                 concern! For in them lie the foundations of my
                 crude conception.

                 Look at me! My scars are written in my flesh.
                 YOU are their cause, and they are the instru-
                 ments by which my every step is mapped.

                 But where are YOUR scars, Frankenstein. You
                 secret them away where they cannot be seen—
                 though they steer you as surely as a ship is driven
                 by a gale.

                 Why? Tell me why you stitched me into being?

VICTOR: Concern yourself with this. I have made you,
                 and I will unmake you the same.

Victor fires his gun.

ELIZABETH: Victor!

The Monster flinches but accepts the shot with a groan, then laughs.

THE MONSTER: You are no almighty god, for you cannot undo what you have made. And neither will you redeem it.

The Monster tears open his coat, digs the shot out of his chest and tosses it away.

THE MONSTER: I am your god now. For in my hand is all your future to give or to withhold.

VICTOR: You blaspheme! I will not hear you.

ELIZABETH: Then I will hear you.

VICTOR: Elizabeth, wait! Come behind me and let me deal with him. His whole nature is governed by hatred.

ELIZABETH: How can the wretched be otherwise, unless by love, or at least by kindness.

THE MONSTER: If I am wretched, it was he who made me so.

ELIZABETH: Then perhaps the twisted iron may be reworked. Come. Speak. And let us see you.

VICTOR: Do not approach her! She cannot bear your odious form.

Elizabeth quietly approaches.

ELIZABETH: Magnificent.

VICTOR: Elizabeth, listen to me!

ELIZABETH: Your form is not lovely, but in your eyes hide storms of pain and grief.

THE MONSTER: What know you of pain or grief?

ELIZABETH: I know of a family lost, and a husband slipping
                 away. What is more human than to feel grief, to
                 suffer pain, to shudder in one's loneliness and cry
                 out for relief?

THE MONSTER: You think me human?

While the Monster and Elizabeth talk, Victor reloads his gun.

ELIZABETH: If my Victor made you, then you must be. You
                 think him cruel, but you know him not. He is
                 kind—and curious and eager—I have seen these
                 in him all his life.

THE MONSTER: He he has consigned me to solitude. What kind-
                 ness does he claim for his creation whom even he
                 cannot love?

VICTOR: Elizabeth, move!

*Victor pulls Elizabeth away and fires. The bullet again strikes the
Monster in the heart. He bears it and roars.*

ELIZABETH: Victor! Enough!

THE MONSTER: Have you forgotten the strength you knit into
                 my form? I do not die so easily as Man. Shall I
                 show you?

The Monster seizes Elizabeth.

VICTOR: Leave her be!

THE MONSTER: And how shall I leave her? Shall I leave your
                 bride as you left mine? Shall I leave you a wife to
                 cleave to, or shall I grant you a torment to answer
                 my own?

ELIZABETH: Wait. Listen. Be calm.

VICTOR: Do not harm her. Please.

Victor lowers the gun to the floor.

THE MONSTER: What say you, woman? How should the creation answer his creator? With the kindness of his natural state, or with the cruelty that has shaped him?

VICTOR: Please! Unhand her. I beg you.

Victor drops to his knees.

ELIZABETH: If the want of kindness governs your heart, then treat with him no more. Look to me. I am unafraid. The charity of the human heart can offer its embrace, even to one such as you.

THE MONSTER: So I believed once, but Man has proven himself unequal to the lies he tells of righteousness. Hatred is Man's answer to the innocent, brutality his gift to the gentle, and exile his sentence upon the desolate.

Your Victor is my maker and my teacher. Look on me and see reflected the abyss within his heart. In his unholy image am I made.

ELIZABETH: You cannot see it, but there is light within him yet. I see that light in you also.

THE MONSTER: In me?

ELIZABETH: Sin invades us all, and goodness is with evil mixed. Yet of a man's heart his sins are not the sum.

VICTOR: Elizabeth, come away!

ELIZABETH: Be silent, Victor!

THE MONSTER: Would that my creator had shown me the
                   smallest portion of your kindness. In that event
                   my ruin might have been avoided, my redemp-
                   tion won, and with it his.

                   But look on him! He grovels like a worm and
                   reeks of his sin. Even now, he cannot love his
                   creature as he made him, and neither will he pity
                   him the manner of his making.

ELIZABETH: Then let us love him till he mends!

THE MONSTER: You would have me love him?

VICTOR: Elizabeth!

Victor draws a knife.

ELIZABETH: I would!

                   To love another who will not love in return is
                   to gain the highest fortune. For it's in loving we
                   discover the amendment of a heart, and not in
                   being loved.

THE MONSTER: You do not understand. You cannot!

ELIZABETH: I understand this: the beauty of a broken heart is
                   written in the scars of which it heals.

VICTOR: Elizabeth, what are you doing? He cannot be
                   reasoned with. Stand aside that I may finish him.

THE MONSTER: Do you see? From death he brought forth life,
                   and now of life he calls forth only death.

ELIZABETH: Listen to me. Please.

THE MONSTER: In his malice are creation and destruction met. His paradox cannot hold—so it must it be *broken*.

ELIZABETH: Please. Let *kindness conquer terror*. These scars can be your glory.

The Monster sobs in anguish, torn between his desire to answer Elizabeth's kindness and his oath to revenge himself upon Victor.

ELIZABETH: Come. Tell us your *name*.

Victor stabs the Monster. The Monster roars, snaps Elizabeth's neck, and tosses her to the bed.

VICTOR: NOOO!!

The Monster removes the knife from his flesh and tosses it at Victor's feet.

THE MONSTER: You are answered, Frankenstein, in the only tongue you comprehend. I shall await the stroke of your revenge.

Victor rushes to Elizabeth as the Monster flees.

VICTOR: Elizabeth? Elizabeth!

Victor shakes her, tries to wake her, but cannot. He sobs, then gathers her up and carries her offstage (as the Monster did his own bride).

SCENE 5

The Inspector enters with Alphonse.

ALPHONSE: Here is the room.

INSPECTOR: She was killed here?

ALPHONSE: He said a monstrous being leapt from the window and slew her.

INSPECTOR: And then what happened?

ALPHONSE: He said the creature leapt again through the window and was gone.

The Inspector looks out the window in thought.

INSPECTOR: A precipitous fall. Would you lead me to speak with your son?

ALPHONSE: He is stricken with grief!

Victor enters, manic. He collects his pistols and knives.

ALPHONSE: Victor?

VICTOR: Who are you?

INSPECTOR: Are you going somewhere, sir?

VICTOR: My wife's murderer is loosed on the world. Wherever he goes, I pursue.

INSPECTOR: Yes. A monstrous beast, was it?

VICTOR: More evil than you can imagine.

INSPECTOR: I would like to talk plainly, sir. At the magistrate's office, perhaps?

VICTOR: It is a tale so strange I fear you would not credit it. You must trust me. And follow. I will lead your men in the hunt.

INSPECTOR: But who can follow a creature who leaps upon buildings or falls without harm? What true pursuit do you suggest we give, if such a creature exist?

VICTOR: My gentle wife lies dead. Crushed in the grip of a monster! If you are too cowardly, sir, then begone, and let better men do your job.

INSPECTOR: I think the monster has, perhaps, not left the scene. Can we be sure he is not in this room, sir.

VICTOR: What?

ALPHONSE: What? What do you mean?

Victor looks around in alarm.

VICTOR: You think me mad. You think I have devised a daemon of convenience and laid upon him the slaying of my wife?

INSPECTOR: I wish only to discuss the facts, sir.

VICTOR: I have given you the facts, sir, and I will not be accused. I confess that William and Justine and Elizabeth all perished because of my actions, but—

ALPHONSE: They what? What is your meaning?

VICTOR: I am not their murderer, Father. I am no monster. But ere I die, I shall be their avenger. Now, sir, clear my way.

ALPHONSE: You will explain yourself!

INSPECTOR: Stand down, sir.

The Inspector pulls out his pistol.

VICTOR: I cannot.

Victor throws the Inspector aside. Alphonse tries to restrain Victor but is thrown aside and falls to the floor. Victor flees as the Inspector fires his gun. Victor winces, struck in the side, and exits. The Inspector blows on his whistle and gives chase.

ALPHONSE: Victor! What have you done?! Victor!

Alphonse exits.

SCENE 6

Victor stumbles onto the empty stage. In the distance: whistles, men shouting, the baying of hounds.

THE MONSTER: *(offstage)* Come, my enemy! We are entered upon a journey and only your suffering will satisfy my rage.

VICTOR: Face me! Do you not dare!

Laughter.

THE MONSTER: *(offstage)* Who now is the creator and who the
                        created? I have fashioned you in mine *own*
                        image! And in your misery I take my sole delight.
                        Come!

The whistles and hounds grow louder. Victor pursues the Monster.

VICTOR: North. Ever north he led me. Down mountain
                        halls, through cathedral forests, across icy prai-
                        ries and solid seas, until at last upon your ship I
                        fell.

The Monster enters.

THE MONSTER: And here we are.

VICTOR: And here we are.

Sailors enter.

CAPTAIN WINTHROP: And here we are.

> You were right, Frankenstein. We are, in many ways, the same. Passion and ambition course in our veins. We might have been friends had our destinies been otherwise.
>
> And you. Though your deeds are brute and your form grotesque, to hear your tale and judge is hard.
>
> Wretched though you are, I confess you claim a measure of my pity.

VICTOR: Pity?

CAPTAIN WINTHROP: Yes, pity! In truth, I pity you both, for in hatred's grip you are equally snared.

THE MONSTER: Then for hatred's sake, let us make an end of it.

VICTOR: Long have I waited to enact my vengeance. Therefore hold. I will wait a moment longer that I may persuade some other of my virtue.

THE MONSTER: My wrath is eternal, and your tales will not exhaust it.

VICTOR: *(to the audience/Captain)* You have heard my tale. You have seen that I am guiltless except in the consequences of my actions.

THE MONSTER: Guiltless!?

The Monster roars with laughter.

VICTOR: And now, as I reflect on my achievements, I rank myself with the names of all great scientific endeavor.

THE MONSTER: All praise the great man! He ranks himself!

VICTOR: My aim was full of glory was it not? I overcame! I achieved what man has only ever dreamed!

                For this my name is raised up to heaven! Do you see it? I shall be hailed as a benefactor of the species, my name belonging to that great company who toiled for the benefit of all mankind.

THE MONSTER: For the benefit of mankind! All praise Frankenstein!

VICTOR: Therefore press onward to the Pole! Do not return to your families in disgrace. Return as heroes who fought and conquered and who did not turn away from the foe. Return and claim your glory.

                But what of mine, you wonder. What of Victor Frankenstein?

THE MONSTER: Yes! Tell us! Let us hear more of him!

VICTOR: My foe is now before me. And I shall meet him. And though he slay me, he cannot take from me my name.

THE MONSTER: Come then, thou faultless god. Let us try your courage. Overcome me and your fame will be complete.

The Monster and Victor square off and circle one another. Victor falters and slips to the deck.

VICTOR: But no.

                   Mine is a great and solitary height, and so must be my fall. My spirit wanes. And like the archangel who aspired to omnipotence, I am descended to eternal hell.

The Monster laughs. Victor's coat slips away and reveals his body covered in blood from the Inspector's gunshot. The Monster ceases laughing when he sees the wound.

VICTOR: The villain's aim was true.

THE MONSTER: What? NO!

CAPTAIN WINTHROP: He is wounded! Fetch him below! Quickly.

VICTOR: It is too late. My life-light darkens.

THE MONSTER: You cannot die! I have not ordained it!

VICTOR: My sufferings near their end. You cannot prolong them further.

The Monster and Captain Winthrop approach Victor, but Victor waves them away with disgust.

THE MONSTER: Stop up his wounds. I command it!

VICTOR: *(to Captain Winthrop)* Listen. That he should live to be an instrument of evil disquiets me. When I am gone, draw your blade and thrust it into his heart. My spirit shall hover near. I shall direct your steel aright. Then with him all my hatred dies.

The Old Sailor draws his knife.

CAPTAIN WINTHROP: Hold!

VICTOR: The forms of the beloved dead flit before me. I hasten to their ready arms.

Elizabeth, forgive.

Victor dies. Captain Winthrop checks his body.

CAPTAIN WINTHROP: He is gone.

THE MONSTER: He cannot die! Not yet!

The Monster embraces Victor, checks his heart, tries to revive him.

THE MONSTER: No! No! NO!

The Old Sailor takes a step forward with his knife but pauses.

YOUNG SAILOR: Go on! Do it!

CAPTAIN WINTHROP: Make no move. Stand back!

Bear witness.

The Monster shakes Victor until his rage turns to grief.

THE MONSTER: In his death my crimes are consummated, and the misery of my being winds to its close.
(to the Captain)
You were right. It was hatred kept us snared. We sought our satisfaction in revenge, and now we've eaten of its meager meal.

Frankenstein! What will it avail if I now ask you to pardon me? I am more wretched now than any ever was, for I have no god from whom to seek my absolution.

YOUNG SAILOR: Kill him!

OLD SAILOR: Captain Winthrop?

CAPTAIN WINTHROP: Your creator is gone, but to confess is to hope for an amendment of life. Speak your peace. We will hear it.

THE MONSTER: When I think on my sins, I scarce believe that I am the same creature whose thoughts were filled with goodness once.

I dreamed that should one being grant me kindness then for her sake I'd quench my hate—and yet I slew her in my rage. I devoted my creator to misery and pursued him to his ruin. So here he lies, white and cold in death.

But my crimes are near complete, and justice needs but one death more.

The Monster turns to the Young Sailor.

THE MONSTER: You! Fetch that timber and heave it onto the ice.

YOUNG SAILOR: What? Me?

THE MONSTER: If you wish to live, obey.

CAPTAIN WINTHROP: Do as he says.

The Young Sailor goes to the rail and begins to throw firewood out onto the ice. As the Monster speaks, he gathers the wood, as he did for the cottagers, and stacks it into a pile.

THE MONSTER: Stow away your fear. For upon this icy waste, I shall collect my funeral pyre and consume to ashes this miserable form.

When the world first dawned upon me, I should have wept to die.

The Monster removes from his coat a flower, the same as he gifted the cottagers, and hands it to Captain Winthrop.

THE MONSTER: Now it is my only consolation.

The Monster retrieves the lantern from the mast.

THE MONSTER: You are the last these eyes will ever see.

> Farewell, Frankenstein! Blasted though thou wert, thou wert my only god and king. My only enemy. My only companion! The maker both of my misery and of my joy.

The Monster gathers Victor into his arms and walks to the pyre.

THE MONSTER: But let us to it.

CAPTAIN WINTHROP: Wait. Is there no other way?

The Monster lays Victor atop the pyre.

THE MONSTER: We are bound, he and I, in cords indissoluble, even by death.

CAPTAIN WINTHROP: Then give us at least your name, that we may remember.

THE MONSTER: My name? I once dreamt of a name written upon a whitened stone—but whatever meaning is in dreams is for some other to discover, for alas, my dreaming ends.

The Monster removes his coat and covers Victor with it. The Monster stands at the pyre bare and exposed.

THE MONSTER: We ascend our funeral pyre to exult in the agony of flame. All vengeful angels shall burn away. Our ashes will scatter over the sea and settle into formlessness—until the sun upon some better world shall dawn. And till that day, far distant and far better, we are embraced—in death.

The Monster thrusts the lantern into the pyre. He embraces Victor as the flames consume them. The sailors remove their hats and cross themselves. The Captain backs away and considers the flower in thought. He puts it into his coat.

CAPTAIN WINTHROP: Could I absolve him, I would do it. His was a singular and desolate grief.

OLD SAILOR: May God have mercy.

An enormous cracking sound envelopes the theater. The sailors stagger as if in an earthquake.

OLD SAILOR: The ice has broken!

SAILOR 2:   The ship is free!

OLD SAILOR: Raise sail. We aim her north!

SAILOR 3:   Raise sails, aye!

CAPTAIN WINTHROP: Belay that order!

OLD SAILOR: Captain?

CAPTAIN WINTHROP: Turn us south.

SAILOR 1:   Sir?

CAPTAIN WINTHROP: You heard me.

OLD SAILOR: But sir, what about the Pole?

YOUNG SAILOR: What about the fortune and glory of discovery?

CAPTAIN WINTHROP: Fortune? Glory? Have you no ears to hear?

> We've witnessed here a wonder, son. And by its dying light, we'll set ourselves some better course than that of Victor Frankenstein.
>
> Bring us around, and aim us . . . home.

All exit.

The End

Also from

Rabbit Room Press

The Battle of Franklin
by A. S. Peterson

The Last Sweet Mile
by Allen Levi

Everlasting Is the Past
by Walter Wangerin, Jr.

The World According to Narnia
by Jonathan Rogers

The Molehill (Vol. 1–5)
A Rabbit Room Miscellany

For more information, visit press.RabbitRoom.com.

RABBIT ROOM
──P R E S S──

www.RabbitRoom.com